MY MOM IS A FIREFIGHTER

MY MOM IS A

By Lois G. Grambling

FIREFIGHTER

Illustrated by Jane Manning

To Kristin, who hung in there through thick and thin
and made it all come together.
And to my grandchildren:
Lara, Ty, Mason, and Jesse
—L.G.G.

To the memory of my dad,
and the members of the Columbia Hose Company
—J.M.

A *special thanks* to the firefighters at the Floral Avenue firehouse in Johnson City,
New York—Capt. Mark Smith (retired), Lt. Mark Meaney, Firefighter Pat Cheevers, and
Firefighter John Fuller—for the help and assistance they gave me in the writing of *My
Mom Is a Firefighter*.

   Thanks also to Robert Blakeslee, Fire Marshal. And to Fire Chief George Maney
(retired), current Fire Chief Henry Michalovic, and Assistant Fire Chief Francis Dohnalek
(retired) for allowing me time with their staff.

   And thanks also to Chris Lupold and Ed Roosa of the Vestal, New York, Volunteer Fire
Department, who provided me with additional information that I used in the writing
of this book.

   Any errors of fact are unintentional and entirely my own. —Lois G. Grambling

My mom is a firefighter.
I'm her son.
My name is Billy.
Mom says she has two families.

Dad and me.

And Marty, John, Pat,
and Captain Mark.

They work with her at the
Floral Avenue firehouse.

I say I have two families too.
Mom and Dad.
And my firehouse uncles: Uncle Marty,
Uncle John, Uncle Pat, and Uncle Mark.

When I walk to school I pass the Floral Avenue firehouse.

Today is Tuesday.
Mom is working.
I leave home early to eat a stack
of Uncle Pat's pancakes.
But when I get to the station, no
one is in the kitchen.

They're all busy.
There was an early morning fire and the
Floral Avenue firefighters were sent out.
They're back now.
But there's still a lot for them to do.

Like hosing down the engine . . . cleaning the air masks and filling the air bottles . . . checking the engine's water tank . . . and washing and rolling the hoses and scrubbing the tools and putting them back in place.

I can see this is not going to be a pancake morning. So I climb the stairs to the kitchen, drink some milk, and eat three jelly donuts.

I
go
over
to
the
smooth
pole
and
get
ready
to
slide
down.

Then suddenly I
remember Uncle
Mark teasing me
about the time the
pole was smooth
AND sticky!
I wipe my hands
on my shirt.
Then I slide down.
"Not sticky this
time, Uncle Mark,"
I say, grinning.

Mom walks me to the door.

"Ready for your spelling test, Billy?" she asks.

I nod. "Dad went over the words with me last night. And I got them all right!"

"Terrific," Mom says.

We hug. And I leave.

I spell the words to myself as I walk to school, just to be sure!

HIKE PLAY FLOAT

After class I hurry home and do my homework.
Mom is presenting a program on fire safety
tonight at my school.
Mom and Dad and I eat supper.
Then we all head back to school.

Mom begins by telling us what to do in case of a fire.

I already know. I listen carefully anyway.

"Get out fast," Mom says. "Don't go back in for ANY reason.

Call 911 and give them the address.

And if your clothing catches fire, DON'T RUN!

STOP! DROP! AND ROLL!

The worst dangers in a fire aren't the flames," Mom says,

"but the heat, and breathing in hot, smoky air."

Mom puts on an air mask.

"That's why we wear masks connected to air bottles on
our backs," she says.

Mom tells us that firefighters are part of a team.
"Everyone has to do his or her job.
And we take turns doing everything.
Driving the rig. Working the hoses.
Mopping the floor. Even cooking."

When Mom's program is over everyone claps.
Then we have punch and cookies.

The next day Dad and I are making dinner
when the Floral Avenue rig races by,
siren screaming and red lights flashing.
I run to the window.
Mom's driving.
I watch the rig disappear around the corner.
I know what my firehouse family will do. . . .

When they get to the fire they'll put
on their air masks.
And grab the hoses.
And enter the smoke-filled building
to make sure everyone's out.
They'll put out the flames.
And smash windows and chop holes
in the roof to let the poisonous gases
and thick smoke escape.

But their firefighter job isn't done.
Not until they *search the building*
and make sure everything has cooled
down and there is no danger of the
fire starting up again.
Then they can pack their equipment
back onto the rig.

Dad's calling from the kitchen.
"Time to feed Polkadot, Billy," he says.
"Be right there, Dad," I say.
Can't let Polkadot go hungry!

After Dad and I finish eating and
cleaning up the kitchen, we hear the
loud **HONK** of the Floral Avenue rig
heading back to the station.

I give my firehouse family time to clean the rig and the equipment.
Then I call.

"Everything OK, Mom?" I ask.

"Everything's fine now, Billy," Mom says.

"It was a garage fire that spread to the house before we got there."

"Have you eaten yet?" I ask.

Mom laughs.

"No," she says. "Uncle Marty was so busy working the radio and phones at the station that he forgot to put our supper in the oven!"

"How about if I come over and take my turn at cooking, Mom?
You and the firehouse uncles can relax while I make dinner."

"Sounds great, Billy!" Mom says.

I walk to the firehouse.

When I get there, I go to the kitchen. I make some cheese sandwiches and heat up some soup.

While Mom and my firehouse uncles are eating, I walk over to Mom's turn-out gear and put it on. It's too big for me. But I strut around in it anyway.

"You know what I'm going to be when I grow up?" I ask, snapping the red suspenders holding up Mom's bunker pants.

"A pitcher for the Yankees," Uncle Mark says.
I shake my head.
"A race car driver," Uncle John says.
I shake my head again.
"Nope. A firefighter," I say, snapping
Mom's red suspenders once more.

"Just like my mom."